## Roles

—

## Location

—

## Time

—

## Maria Callas
Diva. Legendary opera soprano.

## Nadia
Her friend, former „press secretary".

## Bruna
Maria's Italian housekeeper and confidante of many years.

# The island of Syros in the Greek Aegean. Maria's rented house

# The time spent with the three ladies in an eventful meeting.

# Prologue

—

Recording of 3rd act „*La Boheme*" Aria "*Donde lieta usci...*" Callas singing while black and white Photos of her are projected on screens. Then a scream is heard and a voice offstage cries „*Feruccio*".

The lights come up to reveal an ornate bed. We see a man carrying the body of a woman followed by a another woman. They lay the body on the bed. The woman collapses next to the bed, the man hangs his head and sobs. Then we hear the voice of a radio announcer:

**Announcer**

**The voice of the Century is silenced forever. Maria Callas, the greatest soprano of our time, died today the 16th September 1977 in her Paris apartment at the age of 53.**

# Act 1
## Scene 1

—

Greek instrumental summer music in the background. Nadia arrives by boat on the Greek island, it is sundown. She appears in front of the curtain with her suitcase.

**Nadia**

It's been such a long time... just the thought of seeing Maria again brings back  so many memories and so many questions... so much life..., unbelievable emotions... I'm so excited! Her invitation was as sudden as it was unexpected, but of course I spontaneously answered, YES!

How could this woman so grow on me?!  Before I met her, I'd heard and read so much about her tempers and tantrums, that I had no desire to meet her at all.

Pier Paolo Pasolini's producer tried to talk me into working on the film „Medea" with her as her public relations person. I said no! He kept on at me, just to meet the woman and decide for myself. Well I finally gave in and met her with him at her hotel in Rome.

She was very composed and charming. The hotel manager escorted us to her suite, which she found delightful. She then asked to see the rooms of her Maid Bruna and Chauffeur Feruccio. We went up under the roof to the servants quarters. Madame Callas immediately changed and demanded that they be given decent rooms on her floor, or she would move to another hotel. I was surprised! Wow, not what I expected!

She thought that I had been hired as her secretary, and asked if I could take notes of a dictation. I informed her that, this was not my job, and she replied, *"oh well then, someone has got their wires crossed. If there's no reason for us to work together, let's at least have a glass of champagne together"*. I did and ended up working with her after all.

We got to know one another pretty well. (Laughs lightly and a bit smugly.)

I now know the woman more than the diva... although the diva always raises her head when we least expect it. Glamour, goals, gladness, sadness, moments of greatness, years of conviction, of trying...

Not an easy girl to spend an evening with.

If I were in a theatre, this would be my opening monolgue, where I establish who I am... if not, who knows where we'll end up?

Quite simply. I'm simply her friend. I am Nadia, an allround public relations person, a writer and a journalist. Someone who moves in the world she lives in.

While working together on the film „Medea" we became friends, and this friend-ship has continued to grow. After filming the last „takes" in Rome, she decided to stay on for a while to get to know me better, and also my crazy mixed-up bunch of friends.

The first time she visited me in my 5th floor walk-up apartment in the city centre, like most friends, she just flopped onto the sofa until she could get her breath back and whispered, „*how do you get anyone to visit you up here? Those who make it up more than once must be true friends. Do you have an oxygen mask for the older generation?*" Then she looked around and beamed. „*What an adorable place! I think I'll make it up here again.*" Which of course she did!

One of her favourites of my friends was my handsome lawyer friend Marco.

„*I wouldn't mind a little fling with him*", she giggled, „*if he wasn't married.*" Oh, yes, memories... and not the Callas most people expect. Ah, yes, Callas!

Before starting out on this trip, I listened to her recordings again and again, having only really known her since she had all but given up singing. The magic of her conviction, the drama of her voice, the musicality of her phrasing, are just recorded, some time, some where. But the intensity of the sound still curdles my blood and the volume of the voice makes me stop and listen... that's it!

Stop and listen to what this woman has to say... or should I say this Singer, this Artist.An unbelievable volume of music and roles, the diversity never attempted again by any other singer to this day. Her conviction in every role, to every composer and to every moment are monumental.

I'm not even a great opera fan, but I am at every performance in London, NewYork, Paris or Milano that I can attend, to hear all the wonderful singers whose names I can't mention, for fear of leaving someone out.

Only Callas is never forgotten by anyone who has heard of her. Whether good or bad, whether hate or downright adoration, she's never forgotten, except by the younger generation who probably have no interest in opera or her. My nephews and nieces don't even know who she is.

Oops the boat is landing... time to face the dragon. (Grins)

(Blackout)

# Act 1
## Scene 2

—

Maria's voice is heard Offstage.

**Maria**
## Nadia... hello!

**Nadia** (offstage)
## Hello Maria.

The curtains open to reveal the terrace of a simple greek style one storied villa more upstage to the right, leading into the spacious living room downstage left. Maria is seen from behind out on the terrace where Nadia appears greeting Maria affectionately as old dear friends do.

**Nadia**
## Maria, you look ravishing!

**Maria**
## Come, come Nadia, lets not exagerate...you're looking lovely though... In love again? (laughing)

**Nadia**
(Somewhat surprised) **No, just a bit exhilerated from the boatride.**

**Maria**
## Well dear, come in and freshen up while Bruna prepares dinner.

**Nadia**

Oh, how is Bruna?

**Maria**

Bruna is Bruna as always, thank the Gods that she puts up with me!

**Nadia**

Just the thought of her cooking gets my appetite going. (laughs)

**Maria**

She's in the kitchen, I'm sure she'd love to see you.

Nadia exits towards the kitchen as pointed out by Maria.

**Maria**

I left the dogs in Paris with Feruccio, you know how I love my sweet poodle babies, but it's just too hot for them here. (Maria loved her dogs with a passion)

**Nadia**

Oh, I was wondering where they were. (laughing happily)

From Offstage you hear a cry from Bruna and she and Nadia reapear arm in arm, then Bruna exits again to the kitchen smiling.

Maria

I'm so happy you're here Nadia, it was getting really lonesome here alone.

Nadia

Come, come Maria you have so many friends, there's no reason for you to be alone anywhere.

Maria

Well, as you know, there are friends and friends... and I need some time to come to grips with so much in my life... anyway, you run and freshen up and we'll meet on the terrace for a drink. By the way, did you see any suspicious looking types on the ferry?

Nadia

Do you mean some paparazzi Maria?

Maria

Well, you know even here I have been molested by them.

Nadia

No it was just the usual tourist crowd.

Maria

Oh, Good. Meet you outside.

She puts on the stereo with one of her favourite songs „Hernando's Hideaway" and goes out onto the terrace. Lights dim and then brighten again, as Nadia comes into the salon in a cool summer dress.

**Maria**

(From the terrace) **Fix yourself a drink Nadia, and come out onto the terrace, the sunsets are so beautiful here.**

Nadia does that and as she is heading for the terrace the phone rings.

**Maria**

**Be a darling and answer that for me please.**

**Nadia**

(Nadia answers the phone) **Hello, pronto... Oh it's a Signore Lupoli, he wants to speak to Bruna.** (Calling) **„Bruna"...**

**Maria**

(Shouting from outside) **What! hang up immediately! Nadia, hang up! It's that dirty little Greek, he knows I won't speak to him, so he pretends to be Bruna's**

**husband!** (Nadia hangs up and Bruna appears from the kitchen looking puzzled)

Bruna

**Che fai?**

Maria entering from the terrace flushed and furious

Maria

**E lui! Niente Bruna, e sola Onassis il vecchio maiale! That little pig won't leave me alone. Just because marriage to Mrs. Kennedy, turned out to be too expensive for the miserly little creep. Now he's at a loose end again. Expecting me to come running! Me! He can drop dead! Bruna, quando mangiamo?**

Bruna

**Dieci minuti Signora. Ten minutes Miss Nadia.**

Maria

(Back to her charming „hostess" self) **So sorry about that Nadia, let's finish our drinks before dinner. Apart from the joy of seeing you my dear, there is something I would like to possibly run by** you while you are here.

Nadia

Now you have me intigued Maria, what could it be?

Maria

Everyone thinks they can write a book, critique or just a a slanderous article about me...god knows why!? You would think that I was the widow of some American president or something!

Nadia

(Laughing) What do I have to do with that Maria?

Maria

Nothing!

Nadia

(Now curious) So, what do you want from me my dear?

Maria

Nadia, I want you to write my biography.

Nadia

(Astounded) Me, why me?

Maria

Because you're my friend, talented

and I believe that you will actually write the truth as you see it.

Nadia

Is that so important Maria?

Maria

Well... for me yes.. I'm tired of being
labelled the „monster tigress" who
just causes ‚merde' wherever she
lands... Madame. Tigre, Miss Witch,
Miss Bitch! I'm just me Nadia, and I really don't know how to be different...
more acceptable, more sweet, more
whatever... whatever I am not!

Nadia

(Still perplexed) And you want me to write a book about you?

Maria

Yes

Nadia

Why?

Maria

Because nobody else will, as my
friend. When I die, they'll tear my corpse
apart like the hyenas they are, anything to make a buck!! You know how
the press have been after me for years!

**Nadia**

**Okay...** (thinking intensely) **then we have to talk seriously Maria.**

**Maria**

**Good, lets talk as loud and as long as you like, just ask. I'll try to be as honest as I can, whatever that may be...**

**Nadia**

**Okay Maria, I've been dying to ask you those scary questions that wake me in the middle of the night...** (Maria looks startled. Nadia laughs) **Oh, come on, just joking!**

**Maria**

**You see, I knew I could rely on you!** (clapping here hands gleefully)

**Nadia**

**I meet so many people Maria, in my business and travels and they all ask, or tell me about you, knowing that you're my friend. It's amazing the people I have met so far. Do you know Michael Scott?**

**Maria**

(Looking a bit vague) **Yes, I know who you mean...**

**Nadia**

He knows so many of your performances, and is a regular encyclopaedia on your art. Very critical, but very much an admirer of your belcanto... doesn't like it when you sing „verissimo", and „who the hell knows the diffence these days anyway,  as he says. Oh, there are so many, like John Ardoin, Franco Zeffirelli...

**Maria**

Dear John, and how is Franco?

**Nadia**

Full of „piss and vinegar" as usual, and of course very entertaining. ...he loves you very much. So, we should tell your story, your way... I love the idea! Now I can ask you all those „uncomfortable questions that lurk in the dark corners of my mind"... ( laughs)

**Maria**

(Laughing too) How uncomfortable are you going to be?

**Nadia**

Oh we'll see, but I think you can deal with whatever comes your way. (Grins)

**Maria**

I've always had to.

**Bruna**

**Mangia!** (They leave to eat dinner)

Callas singing „Casta Diva" on a recording as they go out with black and white photos of her projected on the set, and fading as they enter again.. the sound of footsteps on the terrace. (Then silence)

**Maria**

So, where do we start?

**Nadia**

„Start"?, like the „Sound of Music"?

**Maria**

What?

**Nadia**

(Singing) „Let's start at the very beginning"

**Maria**

(Laughing and singing) „A very good place to start."... the singing or my life?

**Nadia**

Well, whatever! (Singing) „When you speak you begin with ABC...when you

sing, you begin with Do Re Mi". (Laughs)
For a start, I've never heard anyone as
naked as you...I mean vocally of course!

**Maria**

Well of course my dear, do you think
I'm with the „Folliés Bergere"? Yes, my
voice was always a little naked... oops...
some people say that I sang out of my
vagina! Excuse my French.

**Nadia**

What? You must be kidding!

**Maria**

Well, I don't know dear... it's up to
them to decide. I thought I used my
vocal chords and technique ...but who
knows who's right in the end ? (laughs)
I was never just that...my voice just
wasn't innocent.., even as Lucia goes
mad, it's me....yes, it's always me (she
looks questioningly at something she can't
grasp)... maybe they were right.

**Nadia**

What do you mean?

**Maria**

I'm not sure...Well, more impassio-
ned, at least I never covered my voice,

just to get a warm sound without any real substance...just pretty to be pretty. Life is not about making it sound good, life is what it is.

Nadia

But now, that you don't sing anymore, you're like the „Norma Desmond" of opera....

Maria

Who's Norma Desmond ?

Nadia

„Sunset Bouelvard"... the Movie? (Maria still looks perplexed) A classic!

Maria

Haven't seen it. Well, at least I could sing anything I wanted to... even after „The Voice"... You'll hear... if you want to... and by the way talking of „Norma", I am sure that  Bellini wrote the opera for me. (grins) There are two ways of looking at opera... and me.

Nadia

And what are they?!

Maria

Oh well, yes, from the singer and from the audience!! Those who hate my voice should just not come to hear me sing. Simple, no? I am Norma...not the Desmond lady, just Norma, and by the way, as I said opera is not just about a pretty voice...or a techinique...it's about making it come alive!

Nadia

That sounds good, and what now?

Maria

God knows... on two of my latest recordings, on one I was „Carmen" and on another „Delila", two roles I never sang on stage... but my older self and ‚voice' found a particular way to their souls. And „Tosca", the lady I thought would never really be me, became Callas... now I am Tosca, Norma... both came to a bad end. (Laughs) So, I was born in New York on the 2nd of December 1923... or was it the 4th? In my mother's book, she got my birthdate mixed up, once the 2nd and then the 4th, or was it actually the 3rd? According to her it was a stormy night in Manhatten! The weather report says that it was a quiet normal night, but she always liked a bit of drama,and of course wrote her book to spite me and make money, the „strega"!

Nadia

Why do you call your mother a „witch" Maria ?

Maria

My mother's a very strong personality, totally egocentric, manipulative and unrelenting, something like me. Maybe that's why we never really got on... (shaking her head in disbelief). So, why do I still send her money every month?!!

Nadia

I don't know, Why do you?!!

Maria

I just do!  I don't know why!! I really don't know,  but at least neither she nor my ex- husband Battista will get a penny when I die. I've changed my will to leave the money to a foundation for talented students and to my real „family" Bruna and Feruccio who are always with me.

Nadia

Wow, that is quite a shift! Do they

know anything about it?

Maria

No, I haven't told them. I want it to be a surprise to them should that day arrive.

Nadia

How come you as a Greek girl were born in New York?

Maria

The reason I was born in New York was because my parents decided to migrate there after my brother Vasily died in Greece at a very early age from Typhoid. They were devasted, and wanted to start a new life. So, they took my older sister Jackie and packed up everything. My father, being a pharmacist planned on opening his own pharmacy in New York. Evangelia, or „Litza", my mother was pregnant, and there „I" was, a few months after their arrival, a twelve pound baby girl! She'd been hoping for a boy, that much was certain, so, her disappointment at having me, made her not even want to look at me for four days after my birth... „Too bad Mama, as you see I am still here!" (Gesture „italianlike" with a flick of the hand).

Nadia

You mean that she didn't want you?!

Maria

I don't think so, but I really don't know. The funny thing about my mother was, that, apart from being a snob, she absolutely loved opera and anything „artsy". My sister Jackie was always the slim, beautiful, fair daughter she could be proud of, whereas I tended to be heavy and dark, shortsighted, and as I got older, pimply. Not her idea of a daughter to be married off.

Nadia

So you're saying that she was unkind to you?

Maria

It wasn't that she was unkind Nadia, it was just that she made it obvious that Jackie was her favourite, and that I was nothing! She never hugged or kissed me, to make me feel loved or special, but when she forced my Papa to buy the pianola for Jackie, it was I who first started to play. One day I was playing and singing my favourite song „La Paloma" when a crowd gathered on the street below our apartment window. As I finished they all applauded... Litza plucked up her ears and decided that, even though at that time we couldn't afford it, it was singing lessons from then on. She entered me for every talent contest available. After I'd won one in Chicago, I came in second to an accordian player in a contest hosted by the famous Jack Benny in New York!

Nadia

You mean an accordian player beat the great „Callas"?

Maria

Yes, no need to be sarcastic darling! But I do often wonder what became of him... Oh, Litza got more and more determined... (Laughs) You see, when you have a daughter that's too plain to be married off, she better have a career! Something that I think she had always dreamed of for herself.

Nadia

**Really, so how did you feel about this?**

Maria

**I wanted to please her of course. I knew that this was the only way to do so. There was basically no childhood for me from then on. I got down to it and studied. We used to listen to the live broadcasts of the Saturday Metropolitan Opera Performances and I just got hooked. I also discovered that I could tell if a singer was singing flat or not...something in hearing that helped me throughout my career. I did get that wobble on the high notes later, but I never sang flat!**

Nadia

**Probably not, ...or were you sometimes a just little sharp?** (Grins).

Maria

**Oh shut up Nadia!**

Nadia

**Why did you return to Greece?**

Maria

**My father and mother were not get-**

ting on at all. He liked the ladies, and she wanted to go home, so she sent Jackie ahead and followed with me. I remember, the Captain of the ship we were on gave me a doll when we landed, because I had sung for the 1st class passengers and him. It was the first doll I had had as long as I could remember. I loved that doll! I kept it all through the war.

Nadia

Oh yes, the war.....tell me about Athens.

Maria

Athens was a culture shock for me, after growning up in the concrete jungle of New York City, and then having those glorious open blue skies in Athens, where the sun seemed to shine forever and there were trees and parks and sea.

Nadia

How about the language...was that a problem?

Maria

No, because we always spoke Greek

at home. I spoke english at school and with my friends. By the way, someone once asked me what my mother tongue was, as I lived and worked mainly in Italy and then Paris. I have „this way" of speaking in all the languages I speak....but I did answer that I counted my money in english (laughs... so does Nadia).

**Nadia**

Athens was what really formed you wasn't it?

**Maria**

I suppose you could say so, my puberty and the war, and of course my singing teachers. I began my formal studies.

**Nadia**

At 13.....when did Elvira de Hidalgo enter the scene?

**Maria**

Ah... de Hidalgo... mother heard that this famous soprano who had sung with Caruso, was living and teaching in Athens. So, she managed to arrange an audition with her. She was shocked when she saw me and apparently said. „This girl is heavy and plain and can never be a great singer"... but after I sang she changed her mind. She taught me everything she knew, and increased the range of my voice, my posture, everything she could. I would arrive in the morning and stay till her last pupil had left. She gave me more hope and support than my  mother ever had.

Nadia

Why did you stay when she was teaching other pupils?

Maria

You can learn so much just by observing Nadia. Whether some one is good or bad, there is always something to learn!

Nadia

Was your mother satisfied?

Maria

Well, who knows?  My sister got engaged to the son of a wealthy shipping family and mother was ecstatic...and of course I was plodding along as well.

**Nadia**

Then the war, right?

**Maria**

Yes.

**Nadia**

This time really changed your life as you have said...

**Maria**

No one can understand war Nadia, who has not been through it. I was so involved in my singing and studies that I only discovered the horror on my way home from school... to see and know the smell and hunger, the fear and hopelessness... I was studying all day... then... yes, the war!

**Nadia**

You poor kid, it must have been awful!

**Maria**

Well, we were luckier than most, because Jackie's fiancee helped us with food and rations. The Italians had occupied Greece with help from the Germans who then also occupied Athens. There was a curfew and we were not allowed to go out or make any noise after dark. One night some greek resistance men brought us two British officers to hide. Mama didn't want to of course, but Jackie and I forced her to give in. We hid them in a tiny room where we kept our canaries, and told them never to make light in there after dark. If we had been caught we would have been executed!

Nadia

Wow, that was brave of you girls...

Maria

I suppose so, but, I used to practice at the piano in the evening so that they could listen to BBC radio. Then, one night the Greeks came and took them away again with no explanation. The next evening some Italian soldiers arrived with weapons drawn to search the apartment! I knew that the English had left letters and papers in the room, so I sat at the piano and began to sing „Vissi d'arte" from „Tosca" and they immediately came and sat around the piano to listen to the sounds of their homeland. The next evening they re-turned,  this time without weapons, but with bread and pasta....and so we became friends. This has been held against me, but I don't care. They were just normal young men far from home, doing their duty... not, that they would have had an alternative.

Nadia

(Winking at Maria) A little bird told me that you had an affair with one of them... an officer from Verona... Is that true?

Maria

Oh Nadia, you've just got a one track mind! Well okay, I did like...

Nadia

(Triumphant) I thought so!!

Maria

More important, I started singing with the Opera in 1941 and the Germans he-ard me do „Fidelio" and „Tiefland" and were so impressed, they even organi-sed a tour for me in northern Greece. In 1942 I sang my first „Tosca" with the Opera  Company in Athens, and became a leading singer until after the war, when my „lovely" colleagues finally turned on me, and my contract was cancelled. So, at 21, I decided to go back to New York and my father, and try my luck there. So much for Athens!

Nadia

So, how was New York ?

Maria

Well, to be honest Nadia, it turned out to be a bit of a nightmare.

Nadia

Why?

Maria

I just couldn't find work, and got more and more depressed. Papa didn't help. He had no interest in opera, and was with some other woman. I borrowed money from my godfather, and had my mother come over. She, of course was no happier than I. Their marriage was a farce. I managed to get an audition at the Met. But no contract. They mentioned „Butterfly" and „Fidelio" in english... but I was far too heavy to play a fragile geisha, and no way

# „Fidelio" in english.

**Nadia**

(Accusing sceptically) **You mean, they didn't want you!**

**Maria**

(A bit shocked) **Nadia, you're so agressive! Something I've never seen in you before.**

**Nadia**

**No, not really,I just want to know the truth, if I'm going to write  your story.**

**Maria**

**Who knows?! Then I met Eddie Bagarozy and his wife Louise who was teaching singing, and so I spent all my time with them, working as hard as I could with Louise. Eddie decided to resurrect opera in Chicago and start a new company of european singers and a production of „Turandot". I was to sing Turandot. I was so excited, you can't imagine what it meant to be back on track again... then the artists unions came down on Eddie and the company collapsed. All for nothing... back to despair!**

**Nadia**

Oh my God, you poor thing.

**Maria**

That is, until my friend Nicola, a bass baritone from Verona, told me that the director of the „Arena di Verona" was auditioning for „La Gioconda", and took me to him to audition. He had been planning two famous singers, but after I sang „Suicido", he joined in for the duet and I was „Gioconda". I remeber trembling like a leaf before going out to face 25,000 Italian opera fans... but I did it.

**Nadia**

So, that's how you finally got to Italy, where de Hidalgo had told you to go in the first place. How did it go in Verona? I know that you met your husband there and that he courted you for a long time, against his family's wishes because they thought you were just after his money. You know, that He was so much older than you etc.

**Maria**

The funny thing is Nadia, that Battista

was so supportive and sweet and kind that I didn't even think of money. I knew that he was in love with me, and I felt so safe and protected by him... even after „Giaconda" when I wasn't getting any work, he was with me all the time. Then, Tulio Serafin, who had conducted me in Verona, wrote that I should join him in Rome to work, as he wanted me there for „Tristan and Isolde" a part I did not know, and „Turandot" in „La Fenice" in Venice. My first major triumphs since Athens. After that the offers started pouring in from all over Italy... On the 30th November I sang my first „Norma" in Florence, so thank God for my training with de Hidalgo! (Smiling)

**Nadia**

And that Bellini had written it for you. (grins) Which reminds me of your real „breakthrough" in Venice... tell me again.

**Maria**

Oh come on Nadia, you know the story so well...

**Nadia**

Come on, don't be coy, you know you love to tell it!

**Maria**

But we're not interviewing now... we're just talking.

**Nadia**

I know dear, but I like to hear it directly from you and not from what I've read or heard from others. You're the one who doesn't trust them! You want me to be fresh on your trail.

**Maria**

Okay, okay... I was singing my „Brunhilde" at La Fenice, and happened to see the partitura of „I Puritani" on Serafin's piano... so I sight sang the one aria. His wife was there and heard me. What I didn't know, was that the colaratura soprano who was to sing the role had the flu and had cancelled, and he was desperately searching for a replacement.

**Nadia**

So, what happened?

**Maria**

When he returned, his wife asked me to sing the aria again for him. He didn't say a word. Next morning at 10am I got a phone call from him in my hotel room upstairs. He asked me to come down immediately... I said that I wasn't dressed and needed at least 30 minutes. „No, come as you are" he said, so I went down in my bathrobe. There he was with the director of the theatre, and he said,"Maria sing that aria that you sang for me yesterday". So I did, then they whispered together and he turned and said, "You will sing the role in a week". „But I have 3 more Brunhildas to sing and I don't know this opera". „You can do it" he said... so I said „my best I can do, no more, if you're crazy enough to think I can do it , then why not?!" I was young. The rest is history.

**Nadia**

Yes, and what a history it is! From a „dramatic" to a „coloratura" soprano in one week! Unbelievable, the difference in voice and technique! Of course people who don't know opera have no idea what that means... Boring! (laughs)

**Maria**

Time for me to go to bed, I want to be fresh for you tomorrow. Stay and have another drink if you like Nadia...

**Nadia**

I think I'll turn in too... it's no good you being fresh and me not. (grins)

**Maria**

Good night dear.

**Nadia**

Good night Maria. Is Bruna still up? I'll go and say good night to her as well. (Calling) **Bruna!**

Just then, almost a shadow, a man in a white suit passes through the night in the background.

(Blackout)

# Act 1
## Scene 3
—

Bruna appears on the terrace, on her way to the garbage disposal... she begins to speak, with a strong italian accent.

**Bruna**

I am so happy that Miss Nadia is here. La Signora has been so sad and lonely... Mama mia, la poverina, come sola e abandonata. She misses the dogs, she misses the life she knew....and sopra tutto, she misses HIM (spits)... even though she would die before she admits it. Stubborn she was born and stubborn she will die. I know her so well, tanto tanto tempo. She is a my family. So, I am so sad when she is sad. I remember when I first came to work for her. She was a big star, so very busy all the time. At first she was molto formale and distant to me, but fair and polite, always. It was the smell of my cooking that made her come into my kitchen....so I got my first compliment! Then she start to come every day and always interested in what I was a cooking. She loved to cook, but grazia

Dio, she chose to sing... her cooking is terribile! (Laughs) She was big then and she liked to eat too much... Mama mia, she could eat! Now she eats only „tatar" or steak and salad... she has discipline that woman... She decided to look like the models in the magazines, and so she made basta with her pasta and she became so skinny! This glamour gave her a new life and made her piu famosa  opera singer nel mondo, in the world. She was a great star, one of the most famous women in the world... That was the beginning of  the end. Si e vero... ma che fai?! (raising her eyebrows and shrugging her shoulders)

She hears some one nearby... who could it be? A figure in white moves through the background, scaring Bruna who sees nothing.

**Nadia**

(From offstage) **Bruna...** (appearing) **Here you are, I just wanted to say good night.**

**Bruna**

**A sei tu!** (releaved) **I thought I heard**

someone. Buona Notte Miss Nadia. La Signora is in bed?

**Nadia**

Yes she seemed a bit tired. By the way Bruna, the Signora has asked me to write a book about her.

**Bruna**

Fantastico!

**Nadia**

You know her better than anyone… may I ask you  some questions and hear your  stories about her. Do you think that would be good?

**Bruna**

Sicuramente Miss Nadia… but only if it is good for la Signora.

**Nadia**

Trust me Bruna, I want that as much as you. I know how she trusts you.

**Bruna**

La Signora is no simple woman Miss Nadia, as you know… she is two souls in her body.

**Nadia**

Yes, I think that is the crux of the matter. But who is she really?

**Bruna**

Callas e una forza tremenda... un vulcano, una Diva. Maria, piu semlice e timida... more simple and timid... sad.

**Nadia**

Yes Callas is an amazing force... she achieved everything she set out to do.

**Bruna**

(shaking her head) It cost Maria's life and happiness Miss Nadia, I think... the story is piu complicata.

**Nadia**

Oh yes. Her enemies don't understand her, and her friends don't need to. They love her anyway.

**Bruna**

Si, true friends, who know her... the fans love La Callas.

**Nadia**

Did you ever hear her sing?

**Bruna**

Si Miss Nadia (puts her finger to her lips „hush"), but do not tell her! (adament)

**Nadia**

(Intrigued) Why not?

**Bruna**

She does not know! Except, when she give me a ticket. I used to go to La Scala with my own money and sit in the „galleria" cheap seats. She never knew, mai, never! So often I sat there in the dark and I heard her. I saw her. I lived those nights with her. Every sound, every movement, every tear!

**Nadia**

(Fascinated) So, you can tell me about her, the „Great Callas"! As you know, I only met her after she had all but stopped singing. I listen to her recordings.

**Bruna**

They are good... (nodding her head) but Signora live was a magic of the theatre... a goddess of her art. Sometimes a cruel and terrible sometimes a sweet and apassionata... ma sempre la Divina! She never just sang beautiful notes... she told the story with every note she sang... that was different from what we knew. We listened with our ears only... with Callas you don't just listen with your ears, you listen with your whole body down to your toes, the sound of the soul of the sound... no more just sing nice... tell the story! She brought excitement back to the opera. I cried so often from the sorrow and the tragedia that she sang... but she never knew... don't tell her please!

Nadia

No, of course not Bruna... Wow! You really know her!

Bruna

She still thinks that I am just Bruna the housekeeper... but Bruna knows much more... tanto tanto... e di piu... e sopra tutto, I love music, I love life, I love food... so we meet! Nothing could stop the machine...no nothing... except HIM! (Spits again)

Nadia

Onassis?

Bruna

Si, ma quella una storia diversa... ma... mama mia! She practiced every day from matina till evening... never too tired, sempre... Callas canta... sempre... The voice was never different... it was always her! Always! Good or bad, la intensita of every note... the feeling of every fraze... whatever people say... it was always her. A star, a queen! But for me, Maria... la Signora... there is a difference... she doesn't just sing the high notes... she lives them!

Nadia

What do you mean?

Bruna

The intesita of sound at every level Su, Giu! No one can do this! She lives every momento! And I am the only one who knows what she doesn't. I heard Callas, and I understand and si capito"Maria" , but, who can sing, be, and hold the world in the palm of her hand and make a terrible pasta... CALLAS!

Nadia

By the way, we hear so much of the Tebaldi/Callas feud. The two top sopranos in the world then... or not!? What was the story?

Bruna

It is over... who cares about them now? Who are they? I know only la Signora.

**Nadia**

I know, but I need it for the book. The two most famous singers of their time.

**Bruna**

A si, o mama mia, that was terribile! I think the press and the fans made it happen. The Callas and Tebaldi fans fighting with fists and throwing everything on the stage at the one they hate... eggs, shoes, fruit, verdure... mama mia, they were both so brave to come on stage, and then still sing! It was like a crazy house, but that is La Scala!

**Nadia**

This is really true then?

**Bruna**

Si, One night after the performance people were throwing flowers... Callas, she thought flowers, but some Tebaldi fan threw a bunch of radishes at her.

**Nadia**

Oh my God, and then?

**Bruna**

We know that la Signora is almost blind, but her hearing is incredibile.

She bent down and picked up the radishes and sniffing them, held them to her heart, and then uschita! She swept off stage clutching them to her heart like a bunch of roses. (Laughs)

Nadia

(Really alive and excited) Oh my God, how amazing!

Bruna

Yes, but when Callas sang in Chicago „Madame Butterfly", she told them that one great singer was missing for the season. They said „who"? She asked that one night Tebaldi should come sing in „Aida" and one night Callas in „Puritani" or „Butterfly". She got Tebaldi a job!

Nadia

That sounds a bit incredible... is it true?

Bruna

Si sicuramente... Tebaldi also said that she had no problem with Callas... but the press make a problem for everyone!

Nadia

Tebaldi said that the publicity was

good for both of them. But, in the end Callas won, I hear. After she lost weight and became the „Great Callas". By the way, the most beautiful voice I've ever heard is Leontyne Price.

Bruna

Maybe, a matter of taste as everything... but, Callas she became like a goddess to them... they promenaded her after the opera through the streets to her ristorante calling „Callas,Callas, Callas", with flowers... „la divina"... in-credibile! Then she would say buona notte and go in the ristorante with her husband Signore Battista.

Nadia

(Laughing) Oh yes Bruna, you must tell me about him... maybe tomorrow? Good night Bruna.

Bruna

Si Miss Nadia, Buona Notte Miss Nadia, sognio d'oro... (Bruna leaves)

Fade Out to Black.

Music of Lady Macbeth... Callas singing... black

and white photos of Callas? We glimpse the shadow of the man in white...

(Blackout)

# Act 1
## Scene 4 (The next morning)

—

Nadja enters looking rested and happy.

**Maria**

(Yawning) **Buon Giorno Bruna come stai.**

**Bruna**

**Buon giorno Signora... grazie, tutto aposto, e con lei?**

**Maria**

**Anche, grazie, ma dove e la Nadia?**

**Bruna**

**Non ho visto la signora Nadia sta matina... (Enter Nadia looking rested and happy)**

**Nadia**

**Good morning Maria, buon giorno Bruna.**

**Maria**

**What would you like for breakfast? I only take orange juice.**

**Nadia**

**That sounds great, and some coffee to go with it.**

**Bruna**

**„Okidokie" signore.** (Exits laughing at her own joke)

**Maria**

Nadia I had a strange dream last night...

**Nadia**

Really Maria, what did you dream?

**Maria**

You remember that old gypsy woman in Turkey when we were filming „Medea" ?

**Nadia**

Oh yes... that was really scary! She grabbed your hand to read your palm, then she turned pale and tried to run away, but the translator forced her to speak.

**Maria**

Exactly, and what did she say?

**Nadia**

(Shrinking from saying what she knew) Come on Maria, lets not get into that...

**Maria**

(Adament) What did she say Nadia?!

**Nadia**

(Forcing herself to speak) She told you that you would die young, but without suffering... How awful!

**Maria**

Well, I dreamt that she came back to me last night to remind me of my fate. Then, she turned into a big black bird and flew away... I was terrified. I woke up sweating and couldn't sleep after that... (Desperately) **Nadia, do you believe in that sort of thing?**

**Nadia**

Well, as you know I'm Bulgarian, and we have a lot of gypsies in my country. They're famous as fortune tellers, but I never really believed them, the money grabbers! Some things just really piss me off Maria, and so do they!

**Maria**

Anyway, at least I know that I don't want to get old and weak, relying on the help of others. Nor to suffer some long painful illness on those machines. Please Nadia if that should happen, promise me that you'll pull the plug! I'll do the same for you.

**Nadia**

(Really scared now) **Oh stop it Maria!**

**Maria**

By the way, I want to have a happy funeral and be cremated with my ashes thrown out over the Aegean Sea.

**Nadia**

Come on Maria, you're still young and healthy, no need to talk of dying. (Brightening up) Come on, lets go to the beach for a swim instead.

**Maria**

Good idea!

(Lights fade, as they leave music commences.)

Callas singing „Un Bel Di" from „Madame Butterfly", plus black and white photos of Callas. The man in the white suit passes through after them towards the beach... we never see his face.

(Lights fade)

Act 1
# Scene 5
—

The lights come up again as they return laughing and cheerful from the beach, Maria carrying an old amphora she found under water. She is wearing a swimsuit and a wrap around her legs.

**Nadia**

Maria you're amazing! You swim like a fish! Diving with your goggles and fins and all... Wow, like a mermaid!

**Maria**

(Laughing) Oh, come on!

**Nadia**

You always complain about walking and want drive everywhere, thank Feruccio... (grins) but bringing this amphora from the bottom of the bay... Wow!

Maria starts to laugh as she has sea water in the amphora and throws it at Nadia , who ducks away... Bruna appears laughing at the scene then leaves again.

**Maria**

I just feel so light in the water Nadia... So free! Not like here. There's just no honesty left in the world, not even here on this island am I safe.

Nadia

**What do you mean?**

Maria

**The paparazzi are everywhere, even here! I have the feeling that we are being watched, even now! Isn't it awful to live this way? We must always be on our guard, you too!** (Nods at Nadia) **We possibly give the impression of strength, no tears, no breaking down. Nobody feels sorry for us. It infuriates me! Why the „hell" don't people realize that we are fragile too... Women's tears work wonders! I'm tired of picking up the pieces on my own, aren't you?**

Nadia

(Thoughtfully, Maria notices it) **Yes, I suppose you're right about that.**

Maria

**I should have learned long ago how to cry offstage. But you're right, lets change the subject.**

Nadia

**Okay, we know that you were the**

Queen of „La Scala", in fact there were fans who nicknamed it „La Callas".

**Maria**

Yes, those were the days my friend. (laughs)

**Nadia**

But, now tell me about the Metropolitan Opera, reputedly the „Greatest Opera House" in the world, and your „Thing" with Bing".

**Maria**

My „Thing with Bing"? (smiles sarcstically)

**Nadia**

Rudi Bing is still director of the Met and you are „out"... What is the story?

**Maria**

Well, for my second season at the „Met", I wanted new productions instead of those stuffy old ones, I also wanted to have a steady cast that I had rehearsed with and knew. Not some stranger every night to sing my „love songs" to. Bing refused and gave me an ultimatum to sign my contract. I did not and so he fired me!

**Nadia**

Just like that?

**Maria**

Just like that! I was opening that night in Dallas, so I put on my ermine wrap and all my jewels and went to the theatre. Not an easy night for Callas.

**Nadia**

Oh my God, (sings) „The Lady is a Tramp"? (Maria looks baffled)... „Sinatra"! Just joking my dear. (Seeing her unbelieving face) I hear you gave an historic performance that night!

**Maria**

(Recovering) Oh, yes, never let anyone know how upset you are Nadia. Bing got me out of the Met, but not out of New York! (Shows her fist)

**Nadia**

What do you mean?

**Maria**

Soon after that, I sang „Il Pirata" at Carnegie Hall, with Nicola Rescgino as condutor. In one part he had a tempo that was so fast that I never got it in rehearsal... so he said that he would slow it down for me, but I said to him, you're the conductor, conduct. I'm the singer. I will sing. That night afterwards he said..."we did not have a singer tonight... we had a machine gun!"... Everyone loved it!

Nadia

Oh yes, sounds like a triumph for you. (grins) By the way, I heard an interview with Bing later where he talked openly about your „Thing".

Maria

Oh yes, my „Thing" with Bing... (grins) What did he say exactly?

Nadia

He said, that in his term as boss of the Met he fired two of the greatest geniuses that were ever there... you and Herbert von Karajan. He went on to say, that with you it was a question of who runs the Met, Bing or Callas. „We treated her with kid gloves, but Miss Callas was more intelligent than most artists. You can usually get artists to do what you want in the end, but not with her. She knew what she wanted and would not settle for anything less". So, you really were a pain in the arse!

**Maria**

Yes, I suppose I was, but that's me, and all we're doing is reminiscing... reminiscing... nothing new! Born then, sang that, there... boring!

**Nadia**

You're right Maria, but with a life like yours there is so much to reminisce about. You want me to write a book about your life as it is now?

**Maria**

Oh God no!

**Nadia**

So, how about your time with Elsa Maxwell and the „jet set"? We know that the old lesbian was after you. (Grinning)

**Maria**

(Embarrased) Oh shut up Nadia! By the way, why are you really here? (looking at her intensely) I know that I want you to write a book, but  is this just an interview?

**Nadia**

No, not really, just curiosity. How did

you meet Onassis? What are you up to now? Is there anything left except „reminiscing"?

**Maria**

What do you mean?

**Nadia**

Are you washed up? (sticks out her tongue) Don't answer. Everyone knows about your career, I want to write about my friend Maria, because I care about her!

**Maria**

(With tears in her eyes) Oh, Nadia. You can make me cry... (she giggles to hide it) You touch my heart. Thank you so much... (She leaves to her room)

Outside the man in white passes like a shadow, Nadia turns with a shiver.

Act 1
# Scene 6

—

**Bruna**

(Entering) **Che fai?  La Signora is sad?**

**Nadia**

(Relieved) **Oh, Bruna it's you. La Signora is so often sad these days Bruna, but you know that it is the moments when she's happy that make her so special. She was happy in the sea... like a mermaid...**

**Bruna**

**She was also free and happy onstage. But before, always afraid, in „panico"... but I saw her come as „Medea"... Can you imagine?** (Bruna gets into the mood and atmosphere... an incredible transformation takes place, she puts on the stereo) **She enters the stage, the audience sits up, attenzione! Then she says "Io sono Medea".** (Callas sings Medea in the background, you hear people gasping for breath) **...and then she takes them the whole opera into „il mondo Greco antico". You are in her spell!** (Bruna begins to move as if in ancient Greek Theatre. After she comes to bow Bruna takes the bow as Callas.) **People are standing and a screaming, throwing**

fiori and she cannot even see them, but she feels them... her heart is alive and racing.

Nadia

Yes, Leonard Bernstein told me that her musicality is incredible, as she is so short sighted, she never even sees the conductor and she sits in all the rehearsals of everyone else with her glasses on, to see where she has to move onstage.

Bruna

(Laughing) Si, Tenore Di Stefano told me one day how he was laughing when he sang „La Traviata" with her. Visconti told her to run and throw herself in his arms as she sings „O mio Alfredo". He is sitting in a chair. He said to me, „Bruna imagine if I move the chair, she will run into the wall". Crazy man Di Stefano. (Laughing)

Nadia

Luchino Visconti... an amazing film and theatre director... I hear he went to direct opera only because he was so inspired by Callas. They say he made her his queen... his muse...

Bruna

Si, they were great friends and collegues... They made incredible productions like „La Traviata", „Anna Bolena", I never saw such a wonder on the stage... and more great operas too... but, I think she was in love with him.

Nadia

But he's gay... didn't she know?

Bruna

Sicuramente, and she was gialosa of all his young men friends... especially of handsome tenore Franco Corelli. So much the favorito of Visconti... But, Visconti was sometimes too vulgare for la signora, so she ... "come si dice"... go back... retreat from him slowly... she is quite conservativa. Then, she work with Signore Franco Zeffirelli. They make very beautiful productions too.

Nadia

Tell me about her husband Signore Battista Menenghini.

**Bruna**

He loved la Signora very much... always he was there for her. From the start when she was nobody, till the day she told him to go.

**Nadia**

What was their relationship?

**Bruna**

They were good together, he was older and more, „come si dice"... burgese... provinciale... normale. I think he was not very, caldo, hot, just make business. Always too busy to know who she really was. He just want money and be home. He was not good to be in public. I do not think she was inamorata for him like with Signore Onassis...but he looked after her. He was only very strange with money.

**Nadia**

How?

**Bruna**

He do not like to spend money... "come si dice"

**Nadia**

Stingy?

**Bruna**

Si, la Signora also a bit „stingy" sometimes, but never with Feruccio or me! I think she has no idea of money... sometimes she spenda like crazy, then she watcha every cent. Before she leave him, she found that he had taken much of her money and put it in a bank for himself... he stole her money from her!

**Nadia**

(Unbelieving) He stole from her?!

**Bruna**

Si, can you believe it Miss Nadia?

**Nadia**

No!

**Bruna**

Mi dispiace, I am sorry to say... but that is it. She does not forgive him for this. How can you love a woman and then steal from her?

**Nadia**

(Really shocked) I don't know... I don't understand.

**Bruna**

Because she has no idea about finance and money... she trusts you. How to steal from her? She will never forgive him!

**Nadia**

Oh my God! Come let's go inside, I think she's sleeping. Probably dreaming... dreaming of the glories of the past... poor girl! How do you live today, when your life is in the past? You can't change the past to suit the future. She's so infuriatingly vulnerable, maybe that's why I love her like you do Bruna.

The man in white crosses behind the scenes once more.

(Blackout)

Act 1
# Scene 7
—

The stage transforms into a dreamlike scene. Music. Callas singing "La Sonambula" and large projected Photos of Maria Callas cover the stage... A light mist flows over the scene... Maria appears as if in a dream, like „La Sonambula", one of her triumphant roles "the sleep walker". The music plays softly in the background. She is wearing a long nightgown, her hair pulled back and in a high pony tail. She is dimly lit by side lights only... giving a theatrical and mysterious light. It is as if the „Great Callas" has returned.

As if she were „sleepwalking, the text spoken like an aria.

**Maria**

Callas and me... Who are we? Maria? Callas? Who is she? Who is me? „Callas" the „star", the „Queen of Opera"? Or, Callas the „Bitch" the press call her a witch! Too famous for her own good... She decided to be where she stood... "La Divina"... That is what they called me, and they were so happy to destroy me, exagerate every flaw, every mistake I ever made... Too many for Maria to live through and be happy again? Callas? Maria? I cannot change my name or my nature, which is to be who I am. But the goddess has feet of clay. Possibly, this is what they say. Who are these people that judge me. And what do the know of me?

Changing from the „arialike" to a discussion with herself.

What have I done to them that is so terrible? Am I Lady Macbeth? Am I what I sing? Or should I say sang? Oh yes, they have  dug my grave! Just waiting for me to fall in! Will I ever sing again? Do I have the heart to sing again? (A Pause, and then softly...) My baby is gone.... my man is gone... my life is... gone?! Maria is alone... and Callas cannot help her...

She wanders backstage and the set darkens to her music and photos... Music. Callas singing „Lady Macbeth". The man in white enters as the lights go down and turns the music off.

You never see his face.

(Blackout)

# Intermission

—

# Act 2
## Scene 1

—

The same theatrical situation onstage and Maria enters and turns on the music of her recording of Medea.

**Maria**

(A change in tone... more dramatic...like „Medea" spoken like the role.) **Medea and me... son io... Has she consumed me? I feel her throbbing inside me. I hear her... "The Voice"... The wild creature to be tamed every time I step out onto the stage... Some nights she is the voice I knew. Some nights she will rebel! Only to be controlled with the force, that Callas knows so well.**

**Turning that hungry audience... Hungry for my blood, into cheering, adoring applause...**

**That „challenge", night after night, fight after fright, after satisfying their and Callas' hunger.**

**The triumph of being carried through the streets of Milano by flower-throwing, chanting crowds... "Callas, Callas, Callas"... "La Divina"...**

**The feeling of being supreme...**(Change

of mood and character) **Then the cold sheets of my bed in that dark room. „Titta" snoring in  ignorant sleep, as always... no sex... just snoring... Alone, with my fears and my memories and hopes and dreams...**

**A house with my children. A husband coming home to my arms, so simple.**

**Maria is just a simple girl at heart. A big, plain greek  girl who became  Callas for the art**

**After  transformation into that  creature supreme, I not only ruled the Opera Stage,** (A chnage of lighting) **but there I was, rubbing noses with the most powerful and famous in the world, Ready to be hunted by the press day and night, night and day** (a sigh and acknowledgement) **Loving the attention I was getting without singing a single note! When did I become Medea?!**

Nadia

(Entering, having heard the music and Callas) **Maria, who are you talking to?**

Maria

(Absently) **Callas.**

88

**Nadia**

You're talking to yourself?

**Maria**

Yes, why? (Irritated at the interruption) What do you want?

**Nadia**

I heard the music and then you.

**Maria**

(Maria turns off the music... the lights change back to normal) So what?!

**Nadia**

So, now let's get down to it!

**Maria**

(Turning surprised) Oh my God! Down to what Nadia? (The voice of the diva)

**Nadia**

(Pointing a finger at her) Down to the killing of your art!

**Maria**

My Art? (A menacing sound in the voice) What do you know about my art?

**Nadia**

I know that you were the greatest singer and artist of your time, and now you're just a „name"... a name that only opera freaks know!

**Maria**

So, am I already forgotten? Am I no one?

**Nadia**

Not forgotten, but not important to anyone! You, as a „Great Star" have to know that you are only as good as your last „show"!

**Maria**

(Furious) My last „show"? I'm not a „Show Star" Nadia, I am an artist!

**Nadia**

Yes, and where was that great „big voice" in New York at the „Met" when you came back in 1965 as „Tosca"?

**Maria**

Maybe not so strong, but it was Callas singing „Tosca" as only Callas can!

**Nadia**

I am sure of that! So, now that we know who you are... (earnstly) Where did it go wrong?

**Maria**

(Caught totally unawares) I don't know...

**Nadia**

Oh yes you do! Why did you give up

your American passport to become Greek? Was it so that you could marry him? Is that when it went wrong?!

Maria

What makes you say that?

Nadia

(Totally frustrated) How the fuck do I know, if you don't? Was it HIM? Was it Battista, the man who stole from you? Or was it just your mother who never liked you? Is she the real problem?1

Maria

How dare you?!

Nadia

Oh yes, I dare! Otherwise your book will be nothing!

Maria

Nadia, why did you come here now? Was it just to see me? Or do you have something to tell me too? I have a strange feeling... Lets not just interview me, lets see who we really are, Why are you here? I feel there is a reason behind your coming and your aggresive language. Love or love lost? Is that your problem dear?

**Nadia**

Problem? Are you trying to distract me?

**Maria**

Yes, problem... I can see it in your eyes.

**Nadia**

(Feeling trapped and turning away) Let's not get into it.

**Maria**

Why not, you want to get into me... is it just to divert us from your own story.

**Nadia**

No, of course not!!

**Maria**

„Of course not", means „of course".

**Nadia**

Of course, I want to know why your mother is such a witch.

**Maria**

Yes, my mother is a real and very big problem in my life.....

**Nadia**

So, talk about it and get it out of your system!

**Maria**

How? I've had no contact with the woman, except for the checks I send?

**Nadia**

Why, to pay her off?

**Maria**

No, because I'm a Greek girl.

**Nadia**

How sweet... just being a „Greek girl" gives you what rights? To marry a man you want? To anull the marriage to your thieving Batista?

**Maria**

No Nadia, none, as you see.

**Nadia**

So?

**Maria**

So, what Nadia? What is with you?

**Nadia**

Yes... What?! Nothing!

**Maria**

Ok, I spent my life studying, learning, working, singing, trying to be someone. No one gave a damn! I just had to fight... always fight... never an easy way, never a pretty way, I was never just me!

**Nadia**

So, I should feel sorry for you Miss Callas... The great Star?

**Maria**

No need to. but I thought that we were talking about me, „Maria"... with Nadia my friend.

**Nadia**

That is exactly what I want to do if you let me. I don't want to hurt or demean you... I want your book to be a legacy to the great artist and friend that you are... I just have to provoke you a little and poke you a little... come on, tell me what changed you.

**Maria**

What changed me? Nadia, I spent my life trying to compensate for being ugly, fat and shortsighted, by singing.

**Nadia**

Why singing?

**Maria**

Because that was the only way my mother would accept me.

**Nadia**

(Adament) **So, your mother is the problem?**

**Maria**

(Avoiding the question) **Maybe, but who knows?**

**Nadia**

I don't.

**Maria**

My mother always made me feel un-wanted and a nuisance. My sister is a nothing and my father doesn't really care!

**Nadia**

And who are you?

**Maria**

I am Maria Callas.

**Nadia**

Finally, both of you!

**Maria**

Yes and no...

**Nadia**

Why yes and no?

**Maria**

Because I still don't know who I really am. Who the hell are you?

**Nadia**

Well, when we get down to it... who the hell knows who they really are anyway?

**Maria**

I don't care who they are!

**Nadia**

But, you want people to care about who you are?!

**Maria**

Not particularly. Do you?

**Nadia**

No.

**Maria**

No, now, I just want to be a quiet person, someone who watches the sun go down...

**Nadia**

Oh my God, how romantic... and where is Callas?

**Maria**

Callas is my life and my problem.

**Nadia**

So, the great singer was „fat and ugly"... but the voice of the century... what made you change it?

**Maria**

I am also a woman, I'm an alive human being.

**Nadia**

So am I. What does that have to do with Callas?

**Maria**

I finally needed  to be admired for my beauty as a woman and not just for my voice.

**Nadia**

So, what did you do?

**Maria**

I lost weight and learned how to dress and be beautiful.

**Nadia**

Is  that when the „Great Callas" emerged?

**Maria**

Probably!

**Nadia**

And, the „Voice" ?

**Maria**

„The Voice"... oh yes, even „The Voice" knew of the pain of wanting and needing... Norma, my greatest role, has children, and in her desperation at the betrayal of their father... plans to kill them rather than lose them...

but she cannot do so and sacrifices herself for her children, winning back their father, just to die with him... The children I will never have... I know that now! Callas's „children" are the roles she sang... each one had to be special and alive, never hold back, if necessary give more than you have. Never be satisfied... always strive to do better... a one track life. But Callas is also „Medea", who cut her children's throats in her fury at her man's betrayal, in her unconceding thirst for revenge. Yes, who am I? The music? That is Callas, but where is the heart of Maria? How can I find my way back?

Nadia

(Quietly and very seriously) That is the question.

Maria

(Ignoring her) How could Medea kill her own children Nadia? How could she be so merciless, just to avenge herself on her man and the woman he chose to marry after casting her aside? (An aside) Sounds familiar doesn't it?!

**Nadia**

How can you compare yourself with „Medea" Maria? You are a great Medea, but it is only a role in an opera Maria!

**Maria**

An opera begins long before the curtain goes up Nadia and ends long after it has come down. It starts in my imagination, it becomes my life, long after I have left the opera house. How different am I from the roles I sing?! The press make me out to be a monster. They say I have no heart!

**Nadia**

That's one „quote", apparently from „Tebaldi", after you said that she had no backbone. You weren't very nice Maria!

**Maria**

What are you talking about? Nadia, what is going on with you? Something is not right with you.

**Nadia**

(Avoiding the probe) I know the paparazzi are always after you, but that is what happens to people as famous as you are. They thrive on your mistakes, on your vulnerability.

**Maria**

They said that I was always cancelling performances! I never cancelled a performance unless it was absolutely necessary.

**Nadia**

Okay.

**Maria**

It was just because that time in Rome when I wanted to cancel because I had a throat infection...or at least have an understudy. The theatre said „there is no understudy for Callas"... and of course, that was because the tickets had been sold for a record price and the Italian president and all the celebreties were coming. There was no way they wanted to refund anyone's money! I tried to sing it, but after the first act I knew I could not continue, so they had to cancel the rest of the opera. The press went crazy about me walking out on the president! My doctor confirmed my illness, but it was front page news all over the world. I fought it in court for 13 years before I won the case, then, there was just a small article on the backpage. But, my career was basically ruined by it.

Nadia

Oh my God, really Maria?

Maria

Yes, so, I became „Callas who always cancels"! I have sung nearly 500 performances in my career so far, and I gave everything I had to each and every one of them!

Nadia

I know dear, but it's always easy to blame others, and you love to do that! Why don't you ever blame yourself? You're probably just as full of it as your mother is, your husband, the press... and how about Onassis, hey?

Maria

We're talking about my career now Nadia, not my personal problems!

Nadia

Okay, so your career isn't a personal

problem?

**Maria**

What do you mean? How about your personal problems Nadia? I know that something is wrong! Who was he? Did he leave you?

**Nadia**

Lets change the subject and get back to who you think you are... or were!

**Maria**

Who are you? What went wrong Nadia?

**Nadia**

(Refusing to be distracted) **Try to think. Who the hell are you Maria?**

**Maria**

I am not an angel Nadia, and do not pretend to be. That is not one of my roles. But I am not a devil either. I am a woman and a serious artist and I would like so to be judged.

**Nadia**

Oh, you will be, make no mistake. You are, even now, more of a legend than you know, but who the hell is Maria? Who does she hate? Who messed her life up? Did you fuck your own life and career up? Is that why you always blame someone else?!

**Maria**

Nadia, such language! You're supposed to be the calm one here! Who do you blame for what has happened to you?

**Nadia**

Oh, yes, how calm should I be Maria? You're just not being honest with me!

**Maria**

Are you with me? We'll see! The voice is not as it was... and nor are you. Something has happened with you!

**Nadia**

(Adament) Leave me out of this!! You say that all the time about your voice and what do you plan to do about it? Dedicate yourself once more to your art? Work seriously on your voice and career? Or, are you just going to blame it on others? The „press", for example?

**Maria**

It was the press! Damn them, (looking around wildly at the window) they're still after me! Nadia! Or maybe it's just you! Maybe you're just a screwed up crazy woman looking for a reason to explain why you can't sing anymore!

Maria

You're right. That's true, but you are born an artist or you are not Nadia! And you stay an artist, even if your voice is less of a fireworks. The artist is always there!

Nadia

Where?

Maria

Stop picking on me! I don't know how to find my purpose again....how to go back to what made me who I am... when I don't even know what or who I want to be? Who left you? Tell me!

Nadia

Okay! I finally met the man of my dreams, and he has just left me for someone younger!

Maria

Is she as beautiful as you?

Nadia

(A deep sigh) **He is gorgeous...**

**Maria**

Oh , my God...

**Nadia**

Exactly, for once I thought that I had found the right guy, and it turns out that he is... I know what you want to say! Don't!

**Maria**

(Really compasionate) No, I am so sorry my dear, you should have come to me immediately. Are you sure?

**Nadia**

(Desondantly) Yes, but let's cut the crap Maria. We are here to talk about you. Do you finally want to talk about him?!

(An absolute silence for a moment)

**Maria**

No! How do you know? How did you find out?

**Nadia**

I saw them sitting together in a cafe in Rome.

**Maria**

And? What were they doing in that cafe?

**Nadia**

Drinking Coffee and looking into one another's eyes...

**Maria**

And?

**Nadia**

The other guy was wearing my father's signet ring that I had given to him.

**Maria**

Oh my God, you really loved him! What did he say?

**Nadia**

Nothing. I turned and ran over the Piazza Navona and sat down by the fontana to catch my breath and dry my tears.

**Maria**

And then what happened?

**Nadia**

I looked up, and there he stood looking very sad and gave me back my father's ring.

**Maria**

Oh, my dear Nadia, I am so sorry. How can I help you? What can I say?

**Nadia**

I can deal with it. Just leave it to me and tell me about Onassis!

**Maria**

(Bursting out) I can't! Oh my God Nadia, the very thought of him makes my blood boil and my mind go blank... Maybe you feel the same now?

**Nadia**

You must come to terms with it Maria, or you'll never find peace or have a chance to become yourself again. I will, you know me. I always come up on top.

**Maria**

True. But I am myself Nadia. This is what I've become. I would not be here if my life had been different. I would not have been Callas. How about you?

**Nadia**

At least I know who I am, who he is, who they are and I will survive! Who are you?

**Maria**

I'm a mess.

**Nadia**

**You can say that again!**

Maria

It started as a child. The only way I could get people to like me was by singing. Never for myself. I tried so hard. I learned to work and fight for what I wanted, and have done so ever since... but fighting is exhausting Nadia. You can't win every battle. It doesn't make you a nicer person! Does it?

Nadia

No, but Maria, you are a much nicer person than you let people know. You are strong but fair, fiery but gentle, and so sensitive that it hurts to watch you suffer in silence... not that. You are ever silent for long. (Laughs, relieved at her own joke)

Maria

(laughing too nervously) **Shut up! You're right about that!**

Nadia

You do blame him for a lot, don't you

Maria

No!

Nadia

**Yes you do!**

No! I blame myself for being so weak when it comes to him Nadia. He is just Aristo... he will always be Onassis first and foremost, and everything else is secondary to him. His business comes first and no woman or child can change that. He doesn't give a damn about anything except business!

Nadia

Come on, so what makes him so special? Or, was it his big fat greek dick?!

Maria

Nadia! How can you? Oh, but then of course, you know now too, don't you?

Nadia

Maybe, maybe not, but come on! it wasn't his pretty„blue" eyes! What did he do to you?

Maria

I don't know!

Nadia

Oh yes you do!

Maria

What did your boy do to you?

**Nadia**

Enough... Enough to make me listen to you!

**Maria**

Onassis did what no one could do. He used me as a piece of „skata".

**Nadia**

Come, come, he must have loved you very much, to stay with you for so long. What was it?

**Maria**

He loved the famous „Callas", who added glamour and prestige to his wealth. „Maria" he insulted me so often and treated me as a trophy. He hates opera and called me his „canary"... and said that I should stop singing because he had enough money to take care of me. Not that he ever did. I had one business deal with him...half a ship that sank, and then all of his other women...

**Nadia**

What?! Which women?

**Maria**

Oh don't think that I didn't know! He

had others on the side... didn't you know? That is a national sport among Greek men Nadia!

**Nadia**

What do you mean?

**Maria**

What do I mean? I mean that,at least Jackie knew how to get money out of him! Good for her, because I'm sure he „two times" her. Just as he did me, and that, with her sister!

**Nadia**

Her sister?!

**Maria**

Yes, he was fucking her on the yacht while I was still there, I saw the diamond bracelet he gave her! Then, he threw me out when he wanted President Kennedy and his wife Jackie to join the cruise. He said that he did not want them to meet  his „concubine"!

**Nadia**

Is that what he called you?

**Maria**

Of course, and now he comes crawling back! How dare he?

**Nadia**

(Unbelievingly) **Oh my God!**

**Maria**

**The only reason he married Jackie after Kennedy's death,was because she would be more advantageous to him, Kennedy's widow, what connections!** (Shakes her fist)

**Nadia**

**What an Asshole!**

**Maria**

**Well, my career was going nowhere, and my life didn't matter... I was an old shoe! That bastard, how I hate him! What he made me do... and... no, no, No!** (Breaks down crying)

**Nadia**

**Maria!**

**Maria**

**Finally I can cry offstage... and where does it get me? Can you cry now too,my friend?** (The phone rings... without thinking Maria answers) **Pronto... What do you want?! Leave me alone you bastard. No, I am not crying! Don't you**

**dare! How did you find me here?!** (Slams the phone down) **Can you believe it? How did he know we were talking about him?! He has a sixth sense that one. That is how he does his business... always one step ahead of the others.**

Bruna has come rushing in, looking shocked

**Bruna**

**Che fai?**

**Maria**

**Lui! Stronzo!** (She rushes out to her room, leaving the two speechless)

**Nadia**

(Recovering first) **Onassis!**

**Bruna**

(Nodding gravely) **Si... he never give up, mai, mai, mai. He want her back.**

**Nadia**

**And she?**

**Bruna**

**She love him... she love him too much,mama mia! Better she stay away or he will hurt her again too much. He is sposata, a married man!**

**Nadia**

What did he do to hurt her. Bruna... apart from leaving her?

**Bruna**

He said terrible things to her Miss Nadia, to hurt her in front of strangers... Sometimes he ignore her when there are guests. She sang in Epidaurus in Greece a very important performance for la Signora... he did not even come, but made a big party after on his yacht in the bay. That night he did not even ask her how it was... just asking the guests if the caviar is okay.."more champagne"? I saw her eyes... too proud to cry. Once I heard him talk about her big legs and how she must spend so much money to take away the hair, or she look like a monkey, fa schivo... in front of people! No, no, not a nice man signore Aristo. But she love him too much. Mamma mia! One time she say to me „Onassis won't marry a girl who wears glasses"! Tipico! Lui!

(Bruna exits shaking her head)

**Nadia**

Bruna... I know about the baby.

**Bruna**

(Stops in her tracks) **Please Miss Nadia say nothing about the baby, prego! Gran Dio she will go pazza, crazy! Please Miss Nadia...**

**Nadia**

But, there was a baby Bruna no? In Milano, earlier? A reporter has written that he saw the birth certificate. The baby lived for one day, a premature cesarion birth... he saw the death certificate too... is that true?! Whose baby was it?

**Bruna**

Many things are written about la Signora, so many not true... I know nothing!

**Nadia**

Okay Bruna, I promise I will not mention the baby.

**Bruna**

Grazie, grazie!

She comes back and kisses Nadia's hand. They look at one another, then as one, turn and part...

Bruna to the kitchen and Nadia to the terrace. Music starts. Callas singing „La mama Morte" or Sour Angelica.

(Lights fade)

# Act 2
## Scene 2 (The next morning)

—

Lights come up as Bruna comes in bearing a large bouquet of white flowers... in the background Callas singing the aria from Adriana Lecouvreur „Poveri fiori".

**Nadia**

(Coming into the living room) **Wow, Bruna, what beautiful flowers... where do they come from?**

**Bruna**

**Him! The helicopter just, 'come si dice'... „landed" with the flowers... and a note!** (She exits to put the flowers into a vase)

**Nadia**

(To herself) **Flowers by helicopter...the man is crazy!**

**Bruna**

(Re-entering with the flowers) **Ma, beautiful, no?!**

**Nadia**

**Very.**

**Bruna**

**I remember once before, she asked him why he not send her flowers anymore. He answered „Why should I send you flowers? You belong to me,**

why would I send myself flowers"?

**Nadia**

**Oh no.....but what will she say when she sees them?**

**Bruna**

**I do not know... I will not be here... I go now to the village, shopping. Andiamo con me?** (Beckoning desperately)

**Nadia**

**No, I'll wait here.**

**Bruna**

**Okidokie...** (leaves shaking her head with her hands in the air... the music fades away with her)

Maria enters, looking a little tired, as though she has not slept well.

**Maria**

**Good morning Nadia... have you seen Bruna?**

**Nadia**

**Yes, she just left to go shopping in the village.**

**Maria**

**Oh, good** (sees the flowers) **Oh my Goodness, where do they come from?**

**Nadia**

A helicopter just brought them, and there's a note with them.

**Maria**

(Goes to the flowers and opens the note..gasping!) **Oh my God!**

**Nadia**

They are very beautiful.

**Maria**

Yes, but they're from him! Malaka! He thinks he can buy Callas back!!! He ruins my life, then throws me out...and he thinks a bunch of flowers can buy me back?! (Throws the flowers across the room) He made a murderess of me! He made me kill my baby! he should suffer and die! (Spitting, she has turned into the archaic figure of Medea that Bruna was imitating. Eyes flaming she stands tall like an aveniging goddess, breathes deep.) He will suffer more than he can know! A curse on him and his family.

His children hate me! They say I stole him from their mother! But, she had enough of him before me! I gave him all my love! It was not enough! Nothing is enough for Onassis, no, nothing! His business will dissolve and  he will die alone, unloved and broken... So will I!

Nadia

Maria, stop! You don't know what you're saying!!

Maria

(Crumbling visibly and picking up the scattered flowers, Absentmindely arranging them back in the vase) Oh, I know what I am saying! I know too much. More than anything in the world, I wanted his baby and to be his wife. I would have given up singing in a minute! I would have been the wife that he needed... but when I told him that I was pregnant, with his baby, (stops with the flowers) he said „I already have two children, I do not want or need a baby from you. Get rid of the baby or I will never marry you!

Nadia

Oh my God Maria, Onassis said that?!

Maria

Yes.

Nadia

What a bastard!

**Maria**

I cried the nights away Nadia. How I was torn, between my hungry love for him and the child I was carrying! It took me so long to decide... and my weak female hunger, needed the passion and strength of this man so much that I did the unspeakable!!

**Nadia**

No!

**Maria**

Yes, I aborted my child after four months, to marry him!

**Nadia**

Oh no Maria!

**Maria**

After that it just went from bad to worse... I knew that he was tired of me, but I would not give him up! I wanted this man... to be his woman! Can you understand the longing in my loins, the breaking of my heart? And then he threw me out!

**Nadia**

Stop!

**Maria**

Callas was no longer the „Queen of Opera", „La Divina"! Just a hungry vagina... a beating pulse. I was in Paris that summer...that was when I was in the American Military Hospital because of my acute anaemia...

**Nadia**

Yes, that was when they said that you had tried to commit suicide. Did you?

**Maria**

No, the press were always there, of course. They wrote that I had tried to kill myself. How absurd Nadia, I am a fighter not a dier.

**Nadia**

Oh, I know that.

**Maria**

Hmm... He never even told me that he was marrying Jackie Kennedy. He lied to me two days before.

**Nadia**

So, you were still in touch with him!?

**Maria**

Yes, always... but with much fighting. His butler called to tell me. The poor man, he was so kind. He just didn't want me to find out from the press the next day! Can you imagine how I felt?!

Nadia

Oh my God, how terrible!

Maria

But, as you say, I am a fighter... I got dressed up and Feruccio drove me to a film premiere in Paris that evening. The press after me of course! They asked me what I thought of Jackie Kennedy.

Nadia

What did you say?

Maria

What could I say? I said that I had no opinion, as I had never met her...and now he sends me flowers! He calls me! He wants me back... but how can I? (Desperately) No one treats Callas like this!

Nadia

And Maria? What about Maria?

Maria

(Snaps back at Nadia) What about Maria??! (She sinks down on a chair)

**Nadia**

(Coming over to comfort her) **I care about Maria... I will write your book my friend  Maria... but you must face your demons and deal with Onassis on your own! Just as I must... and I will.**

**Maria**

(Desperately) **How Nadia? How? How do you deal with life and love?**

**Nadia**

**I don't know Maria. I love to fall in love and have sweet and sour love affairs... but something like this I have never known.  Not even with him... Your passion is too deep. Do you really still love him?!**

**Maria**

**Can love ever die? Can I ever be free? I wake at night wet with passion and sweat! I feel his trobbing inside me! I know his weakness and his strength, like no one else, and he knows this! No other woman  could give him what I can and did... So why did he throw me away? Why Nadia? Because he is a monster and an egotist, and so viri-**

le and wild that I can die of longing...
I despise him and I want him and I hate
him and I love him and I smell him and
I feel him and I cannot forgive him!
I killed my life, my baby, for him! Now
I am just a shadow Nadia. I walk and
talk and laugh and drink and eat my
stupid steak tartar with salad, and
watch the sunset. I listen to my recordings and know, „Callas will never sing
like that again". I am a shadow Nadia,
the shadow of my life, my art, my music... if only I still had my  music.

Nadia

You will always have your music Maria, that is you.

Maria

(Thinking deeply) That's true, but music without love? The love of a man, of
a mother, of yourself... of your child?
To hold my baby in my arms and sing
it to sleep with the sweet lullaby of
a mother... a mother who loves her
child more than life... something I never knew. Something I will never know.
Please Nadia, find yourself a good

man, make him happy and give him babies... Loneliness is the slow death I am living. Loneliness... loneliness... don't you do the same...

Nadia

Maria, you need to build your life again, whether you sing or not, be alive and embrace your true friends and your own beauty again. You are a very special person. You have given the world so much beauty and pleasure. So many great atrists love and admire you. You are larger than life. Dive into the ocean and swim if you must, but come out alive again. You need to work again.

Maria

(Resigned) They have asked me to give a series of „Master Classes" in Juilliard... you could write a play about that! (Laughs bitterly) But, the pain in my heart is too much to bear Nadia, I'm drowning more than swimming... I listen to the last act of „Traviata" again and again... what I acted onstage is becoming more and more just me... I feel that I am dying. It is just a matter of time. A matter of loneliness. Just the song from my heart.

Nadia

You just told me five mnutes ago that you're a fighter, not a dier... so fight Maria, fight!

Maria

I also told you that fighting is exhausting. I am so tired Nadia. So tired of the fight I have fought all my life... Fighting for the love of my mother, which I never had... or felt? Fighting for my music, against a world used to listening differently. Fighting to be beautiful when I hated my fat body. Fighting for the man I loved too much and too blindly... Fighting, fighting, fighting... I am tired, I am dying... but, slowly, as you know, after all, „I am a fighter".

(She suddenly laughs... Nadia laughs with her)

Nadia

Don't tell me that in your „dying fight" you're developing a sense of humour?!

Maria

(Still laughing) God knows, but it does

**feel good to laugh.**

Bruna peeks around the door with her shopping, having heard the laughter.

**Bruna**

**Tutto a posto? All okidokie?** (Grins)

Seeing her worried face sets the two of them off again laughing hysterically... she joins in.

**Maria**

**What's for lunch Bruna? How about some salad and steak tartar for a change?** (They start laughing again)

**Bruna**

**E un po di vino rosso, no?** (Laughing with them)

**Nadia**

**Yes, how about some Lambrusco?** (Giggles on)

**Maria**

**And so we live to fight another day!** (Grinning from ear to ear)

**Nadia**

**But, I think we deserve an ice-cream**

after lunch.

**Maria**

**Oh yes! Now you're talking!** (The phone rings) **No, not again!**

**Nadia**

**Let me...** (Answers the phone) **Hello... Oh, hi Mani, how are you? Fine thanks and you? Yes, she's here, do you want to talk to her? It's Mani for you.**

**Maria**

(Taking the phone) **Ela Mani, ti kanis? Kala, I am fine thanks... Yes... No! How do you know?! When? No! Are you sure? And she? She's not with him? He is alone on the boat?! When does he set sail? Mama mia!! Please Mani organise the helicopter, we must leave here as soon as possible... Why tomorrow morning?! Not earlier?! But he will arrive here tomorrow... Are you sure? Please, just make sure that we leave before he gets here! Ok, I'm relying on you! Efxaristo poli Mani!** (Hangs up) **Time to go girls!**

**Nadia**

**What happened?**

**Bruna**

Chi fai?

**Maria**

Onassis is on the yacht on his way here!

**Nadia**

Oh my God!

**Bruna**

Gran Dio!

**Maria**

Let's pack. (Exits to her room)

**Nadia**

(Calling after her) Maybe it is time to face him!

**Bruna**

No Miss Nadia, no! Time to go! She cannot face her „destino" like this. He is her death... la morta! He is her life that was. He is a terribile thing that follows her till she die! If she want to live... She must go! (Exits)

(Lights fade to black)

Enter the man in white, he puts on the last act of „La Traviata".

# Act 2
## Scene 3 (The final scene)

—

The lights come up again in the same dreamlike scene as earlier with black and white photos of Callas. The last act of „La Traviata" plays... as the lights fade up to dawn, we see Maria sitting despondantly surrounded by her luggage in the semi dark room.

**Maria**

(Quietly) **Here I sit alone with my thoughts. Am I alive? Or am I dead? Nadia is right. The world does not revolve around me... believe it or not.** (A sighing grin) **I thought I could change things... But who the hell listens to opera anymore anyway? Yet, it's the only way I know how to tell the story. So, where did I go wrong? I wanted to be loved for who I was and not what I was? I spent my life creating Callas, and in my vanity I destroyed her within a few years. Because of my very real need just to be a woman, which is not a crime, unless you destroy yourself in the process... And, who gives a damn except you?** (Nadia and Bruna enter with their luggage, standing silently in the background listening) **My vanity made me famous and  I gave myself over to the pleasures of love and fame.** (Half to Nadia and Bruna) **I never had the technique in life that I had in my voice!**

**How could Callas have felt every emotion, every feeling, every need of every woman she sang? Their pain, their joy, their love, their hate, no one could express it like Callas! Was Maria even listening? How could I fall into the trap of so many of my heroines? I picked the wrong man. He did not know or even care who I really was.**

**It is not his fault. He is who he is. Now he is coming for me, the smelly greek... sailing on his boat. The passion of our love will never die. But, he is still married, and if I'm not dead, I have a life to live, wherever it goes... Nadia, only once he said to me... I do not love you as you desereve to be loved, but I love you the only way I know how.** (The sound of an approaching helicopter)

**Nadia**

**Mani is here.**

**Bruna**

**Andiamo Signora.** (She goes out taking Maria's luggage, returning to help Maria. The sun is rising and the house begins to fill with light. Maria just sits staring in front of her. She finally gets up to exit with Bruna)

**Maria**

**Come Nadia... time to face the world again.** (Exit)

The man in white enters as the lights fade and beginsand puts a white flower into the vase.

The End.

# Epilogue

—

**5 years after Maria's death, Nadia meets Bruna again in her village.** (They approach one another carefully at first, then emotions take over and they run into one another's arms.)

Nadia

**Bruna, I am so happy to see you again!**

Bruna

**Anch'io Miss Nadia, anch'io... and your book?**

Nadia

**I am nearly finished. I have been researching and writing, but am still missing information. I have thought of you and Feruccio so often, but did not know where to contact you. Finally I thought of your home town. Are you in contact with Feruccio?**

Bruna

**Not for a long time now... he seems to have... come si dice... disappeared.**

Nadia

**Why Bruna?**

**Bruna**

I think the shock was too much for him.

**Nadia**

The shock of Maria's death?

**Bruna**

Si, and what happened after.

**Nadia**

What happened?

**Bruna**

Strange things, not good! Many strange people arrive and Signore Battista anche.

**Nadia**

Menenghini?

**Bruna**

Si, immediamente, and a „Signora pianista", she organise everything. People take la Signora's clothes, papers, totalmente confusione... Arriva Signora's sister, half the dresses already gone.

**Nadia**

(Almost to herself) Ah, yes, the vultures, just like she said...

**Bruna**

They lay Signora out like a queen

on her bed, then they take her personal moments and life in their greedy hands! My body is trembling with shame and tears... Feruccio he run from the apartment! I never knew such a sorrow Miss Nadia!

Nadia

You know that Signora loved you and Feruccio like her family.

Bruna

Si Miss Nadia, we knew her too well. We lived her loneliness and her greatness with her. We knew the high and low times with her. (Shakes her head) After Signore Onassis he die, she lose all interest in life. Just watch the televisione, take pills to sleep... una tragedia... listening to her old recordings.

Nadia

I am so sorry that you had this time with her, but I am happy she left you money in her will.

Bruna

(Surprised and shocked) **Money?!**

Nadia

Yes, she told me in Greece, she had

changed her will, so that you and Feruccio would inherit money.

**Bruna**

E vero?! No, Miss Nadia we got nothing, nothing at all...

**Nadia**

(Shocked) **What? How can that be?!**

**Bruna**

I do not know Miss Nadia, but Feruccio and I, they told us to go...no more. Signor Battista and la Mama di Signora, they get the money. The Testament say so.

**Nadia**

Who told you to go?

**Bruna**

Signore Battista and „la Pianista".

**Nadia**

Oh my God! They even stole her last wishes and the will. That was the old will and testament when she married him Bruna! Battista had a copy!

**Bruna**

(Suddenly lighting up) **Miss Nadia, you know something? You make me so happy today.**

**Nadia**

(Surprised) **Happy?!**

**Bruna**

**Just to know that la Signora thought to give Ferucco and me her love. Money alone is nothing without love!**

**Nadia**

**Bruna you are not a housekeeper, you are a philosopher.**

**Bruna**

**No Miss Nadia, just a simple, and now a happy old woman.** (Pointing up) **Signora, I kiss your eyes. Thank you for your love.**

**Nadia**

(To her invisilble friend) **Maria... it's incredible... even after you're gone, you're still not an easy girl to spend an evening with...** (A big smile)

The End.

Kevin Oakes, born in Johannesburg, South Africa, grew up in a musical family in Hermanus, near Cape Town. His mother a soprano with a beautiful voice taught him to appreciate classical music. Having heard and been inspired by Maria Callas he went to Europe at the age of 18 to study opera. Instead of completing his musical studies he attended the „Hochschule für Musik und Darstellender Kunst" in Frankfurt, Germany and studied drama. He then performed in State theatres in Frankfurt and Heidelburg, the Bad Hersfeld Festspiele, also in English with the American theater company „The Company". He then went on to found the now „Frankfurt English Theatre", the largest English language theatre on the European Continent, where, after one year under his artistic direction, where he directed 5 plays and starred in 3, the city of Frankfurt agreed to the first subsidy for the theatre. Kevin then moved on to found „Fragile Theatre" in London, where his first play „Orestes" was performed, followed by Amsterdam, Frankfurt and Hamburg with his new company. His next 3 plays „Ut-Chinkaa" (The Journey), „Too Wilde for Words" on the life of Oscar Wilde and „Raw Knees" an anti war play were performed throughout Europe and even down to Cape Town's anti apartheid theatre „The Space". The theatre piece „Song of the Sands" , based on his short stories with music, dancers and art was performed in the „Gallus Theater" in Frankfurt in 2019, before COVID. „Callas and Me" is his latest work.

„*Callas and Me*" a play by Kevin Oakes

Fact meets Fiction.

For the mental and creative support Susa Pflug

For the graphic implementation moka.

All rights belong to the author Kevin Oakes

Published by Susa Pflug

**M I E T S C H O U**
m u s i c / b o o k s

Herstellung und Verlag: BoD – Books on
Demand, Norderstedt
ISBN: 9783759759542